Coughler

Bearcub and Mama

For my children, Adrian, Guy and Mia DiLena — S.J.
For Elisa — M.W.

Kids Can Press acknowledges the financial support of the Government of Ontario, through
the Ontario Media Development Corporation's Ontario Book Initiative; the Ontario Arts
Council; the Canada Council for the Arts; and the Government of Canada, through the
BPIDP, for our publishing activity.

Published in Canada by   Published in the U.S. by
Kids Can Press Ltd.   Kids Can Press Ltd.
29 Birch Avenue   2250 Military Road
Toronto, ON M4V 1E2   Tonawanda, NY 14150

www.kidscanpress.com

The artwork in this book was rendered in acrylics, on canvas.
The text is set in Souvenir.

Edited by Tara Walker
Designed by Karen Powers
Printed and bound in China

This book is smyth sewn casebound.

CM 05 0 9 8 7 6 5 4 3 2 1

National Library of Canada Cataloguing in Publication Data

Jennings, Sharon
    Bearcub and Mama / written by Sharon Jennings ; illustrated by Mélanie Watt.

ISBN 1-55337-566-1

1. Bear cubs — Juvenile fiction. I. Watt, Mélanie, 1975– II. Title.

PS8569.E563B42 2005   jC813'.54   C2004-902477-9

Kids Can Press is a **CORUS**™ Entertainment company

Bearcub
and Mama

Written by **Sharon Jennings**   *Illustrated by* **Mélanie Watt**

KIDS CAN PRESS

Bearcub always knows where his mama is.

He knows because Bearcub follows his mama wherever she goes. Down to the river, across the meadow, Bearcub follows his mama.

By Mama's side, Bearcub discovers how
to catch a fish and how to dig for grubs.

With Mama's help, Bearcub learns to climb
a tree. *Try again*, Mama urges him. *Try again*.
And one day, high, high up, Bearcub finds
honey. *Bears have a sweet tooth*, says Mama.
Bearcub learns she is right.

Every day, through spring and
summer, Bearcub grows with Mama.
And every night, in the dark,
Bearcub rests beside her.

In the autumn, bigger and stronger, Bearcub sometimes leaves his mama. He plays in the waterfall he has discovered. He feasts in the cornfield he has found.

One day, Bearcub finds something new. Up in the high country — a sheen of frost upon the ground, fragile ice along the shore.

Bearcub slips and skids and splashes.
One snowflake falls, then two and three and four. Bearcub growls his surprise.
Lunging and twirling, he doesn't see the clouds darken. He doesn't feel the wind blow cold.

When the storm spills out of the sky,
Bearcub wants his mama.

He stands and howls as Mama taught
him to do. But he cannot see, and the
cries of the wind are louder than his.

Bearcub drops to the ground.
He hides his eyes with his paws.

But Mama will worry, Bearcub
thinks. And he knows to go home.
   He twists and turns to catch his scent.
He sniffles and snuffles to follow his trail.
   At last the trees are familiar, the rock just so.

Into his den Bearcub scrambles. But Mama is not there.
Bearcub whimpers and turns around and around. Mama does not come.
Bearcub lies down on the branches and leaves and moss of his bed.
His mama's scent surrounds him.

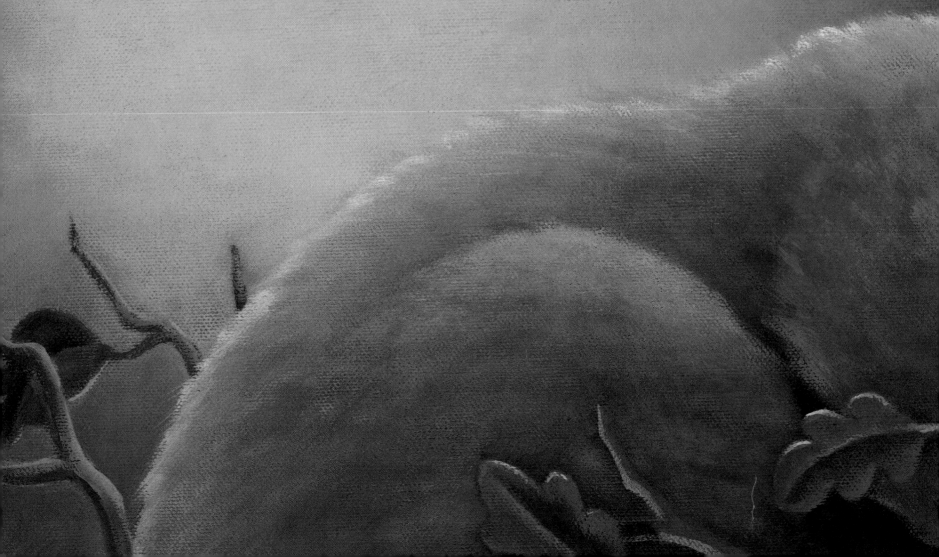

Then Bearcub remembers another day, when he and Mama
found berries, when thunder and lightning ripped open the sky.
All storms pass, said Mama.

Bearcub shuffles further into his bed and sniffs, nose deep
in the branches. He hums as Mama taught him to do.
He remembers her strength and he remembers
her warmth and he remembers all of
the lessons he has learned.

And in the morning, Mama
is there, poking and prodding
and licking her cub.

I remembered, Bearcub
tells her. *All storms pass, and
I remembered.*

Bearcub always knows where his mama is.
She is with Bearcub, forever and ever.